Michael's First Real Christmas

Written by Marion W. Richardson

Illustrated by

Marion W. Richardson
Kat Ford
3660 Highway 41
Stanley, New Mexico 87056-9708

ISBN-13: 978-1494272791
ISBN-10: 1494272792
First Edition

And this shall be a sign unto you; Ye shall find the babe wrapped in swaddling clothes, lying in a manger.

Luke 2:12 (KJV)

Michael had waited for so long to participate in the annual Christmas Pageant. "Not until you are old enough," his mother had told him. "Perhaps next year," asserted Ms. Nancy, the director. While his father simply patted his head with a sympathetic, "Your day will come, son."

And sure enough, his day *had* arrived! So why his disappointment?

Michael sat, cross-legged and balancing a glassy green bottle on his right leg. "Frankincense," he murmured. "I waited all this time to bring Frankincense."

Robert Drake hovered over a make-shift manger. His blonde curls and freckles did not match the image Michael had of the Joseph character. Yet, he was impressed that Robert got to be a carpenter.

Felicia Sanchez knelt beside Rob, acting out her role as Mary. She'd just gotten new braces. Their red and green bands shone like holly berries when she smiled.

Kendrick Watson and Stu Erickson were the shepherds. "Lucky boys," quipped Michael. "They have cool wooly sheep and awesome staffs. Wise men carry sissy gifts. What baby wants oil?"

As he surveyed his fellow cast members, Michael kept his face low so no one saw his furrowed frown. By the end of his ranting, the only role he had not critiqued was that of The Christ Child. The rubber dolly lay quiet in perfect performance. Undeniably, this still and lifeless form wrapped in simple flannel, held the lead part in the pageant.

He had been so busy grumbling about his own bad fortune that Michael missed the signal introducing the final song. From around the auditorium, voices chimed as the cast gathered around the spot-lighted manger. Sarah Rose Watson, as angel Gabriel, swung her hands up, indicating for the audience to join in. "Go Tell It On The Mountain," they joyously bellowed.

"Finally," Michael blurted to the nothingness he had built around himself. "I am ready for a REAL Christmas," he thought in anticipation. Michael's eyes twinkled and a grin grew upon his lips as the REAL Christmas world beckoned him home!

Michael bounded eagerly through the open door. He leaped the rounded basset hound snoozing in a lump at his feet. In a flash, he had thundered down the tiled entry toward the twinkling lights at the back of the house. "Now *this* is Christmas!" he exclaimed. As he scooped up a handful of glistening silver balls, he flung himself into the softness of a cushion lined sofa.

Michael drew in a deep long breath. "Ahhhh." A whiff of the piney tree scent mingled with the hot plastic aroma drifting from the strings of colored lights instantly enveloped Michael. The enchanting balm blanketed his exhilarated mind and wooed him tenderly.

"Welcome, Christmas," Michael sang. He was satisfied for the first time this night.

With precision, ritual began. First, fresh, soft cookies, drizzled with sugary icing, the best of the batch, were positioned on an heirloom china dish. Since he was old enough to remember, the family had arranged three cookies and a fresh carrot on this red plate.

Beside the plate, a mug of freshly poured milk was placed. It's froth bubbled up to the rim.

Santa worked hard and would be thirsty, Michael reasoned.

Finally, and most essential, was the note for Santa. Michael's recently perfected cursive writing had won him the honor of penning the highly prized message.

"For Santa," it would read.

Intently, Michael picked up the pen, positioning its tip over the nappy parchment card. He pressed his tongue against his quivering lip, rested his arm on the table edge, and lowered the pen. "Fooooo-r Saaan-taaa," he voiced.

"For Santa," he wrote.

For Santa," he read.

Yes, all letters were perfect! "For Santa!" he squealed
as he dropped the pen and high-fived the air.

With expectation, Michael's muscles moved him toward his bedroom. He took one last peak at the colorful twinkling beacons which would direct Santa's tinkling team of reindeer.

The woodsy glow crept down the hall where it reminded Michael of a campfire's frolicsome coals. The faint light was just enough to assure him that it was all very REAL.

Christmas was here and Michael was a part of its REAL-ness.

Cuddled under a cotton blanket with Teddy tucked tight under his arm, Michael drifted off into a deep sleep. Eight was the earliest he was could get up in the morning so he did not struggle with the worry of over sleeping.

He drifted off to sleep under the downy covering. Morning would arrive soon.

As the clock ticked on, Michael's grip loosened on the bear and found the raveled edge of his blanket. It was worn thin, soft, and smooth from years of caressing. Michael moved his fingers along the fibers while, in his sleep, Michael's dreaming brain traveled to another blanket.

Michael's touching of his own blanket had drawn him back to the blanket from the pageant and into the distant world where an actual blanket enveloped The Christ Child. There the baby Jesus lay in a manger, wrapped in a simple cloth.

Jesus lay still as he slept. Around his head radiated a glowing circle of light. It was not much unlike the one Michael's tree had emitted, only it did not smell of melting plastic.

The piercing brightness fused with a web of soft hovering light created a haze of fog that resonated colors of majesty. Michael felt as though it spoke. He heard it say, "GLORY".

Tangled in this ethereal mist, Michael could not move. He would not even if he could. An overwhelming desire overcame him to remain in this tranquility forever. It made him feel so REAL.

As his eyes adjusted, he came to focus on other figures in the setting. Bleating lambs, nested with ewes in the fresh heaps of golden straw. Beside them, oxen snorted, moving the hay around for a comfortable night's rest.

A duo of donkeys nudged at each other, their ears flickering in the gentle night breeze.

A more humble setting had never been staged for the arrival of a more regal guest.

As he continued to dream, Michael saw other characters before his sleeping eyes.

There were shepherds in long cloaks whose warp and weft was made of hand dyed wools sheared from the flock. Their faces showed awestruck wonder as they gazed upon the *Miracle Of Heaven* who had been brought into their world of hilly fields. Who could have predicted the wonderment that had invaded their lives this night?

The shepherds knelt before the parents of the babe snuggled with linen wrappings. Joseph, the earthly father, was only beginning to appreciate the greatness of the arrival of this King of kings into his meager family's realm.

Kneeling beside the make shift beddings was the mother of The King. Devotion and love shone on her face as she gazed loyally on this Holy creature whom she had birthed this night. A solemn far-off look filled her eyes as she stroked the baby's smooth skin. She was absorbed in the moment. One could only imagine what she pondered.

For the second time this Christmas Eve night, Michael found himself cross-legged with a company of kings. He crouched, not on a carpeted stage, but on a barren dirt floor of an adobe homestead.

Alone from the corner, Michael could see figures beneath the lintel of the door. Their apparel was foreign with tall hoods, thick robes, and strands of jewels.

Michael watched as the first of the men held up his treasured box to the mother, Mary, then placed it in her quivering hands. As tears puddled in her eyes, a dark skinned man came forward. He raised a heavily carved inlaid chest over his head, recanted eloquent words, then laid the box reverently in Mary's waiting arms.

Past the door, Michael could see the towering silhouettes of camels. Their heads nodded as their shaggy legs restlessly shifted their weight, first to the left, then to the right. Long eyelashes batted in rhythm as their jowls munched on scattered oat grains.

They were as adorned with fine velvety fabrics as the cargo they carried. Starlight lit the camp of a great caravan bustling with energy and anticipation. They all waited patiently as if this were the most important journey of their lives.

It did not occur to Michael, in his dream state, to wonder why the sky was so brilliant. The visitors knew; however, for they had followed the star far. Ancient texts had made them aware of the importance of the child-king they had come to witness.

Michael saw one last royal figure approach the still reflective Mary. He carried a treasure that must have been of great value for he held it as though it were a bird's egg. He laid it at the bed of the young Jesus whose attentive eyes were fixed on the curious visitor.

The final foreigner laid his extravagant liquid before The Messiah. He knelt and bowed low to the child. This scholarly gentleman's grimace disclosed his feelings of insignificance concerning the gift he was presenting. His gift appeared so small before this Creator of all creation.

He turned and shuffled off with regret that he had not spoken. His tongue longed to speak, "Though Eternal and Righteous King, Praise Your Holy Name."

Michael sat in the shadows and took it all in. How is it that a boy of eight could see and know what was happening without ever being told? This night, Michael saw Christmas for the night it IS, the night that God sent His Son to earth to save mankind. This was the REAL thing!

Morning came. Michael's parents listened for the sound of his footsteps pounding down the hall. Eight o'clock had come. Where was Michael? Had he forgotten Christmas?

In his room, Michael felt the sunlight stream through the spaces in his curtains. As a single ray struck his left eye, his brain fought between the world of dream and the world of day. The daytime world won out for the presents called from under the tree.

Michael jumped, no leaped, no flew out of his bed. Like a streak of lightening he was down the hall and surrounded by packages. They were innumerable! Oh, how faithful Santa had been. The snacks must have been just right this year. The cursive note must have wooed them, as the toys were so unbelievably just what Michael wanted.

With his shining airplane with REAL sound effects, Michael zipped up and down the hall wearing a REAL cowboy hat and chaps, toting a REAL action figure with REAL artillery. "Oh, thank you, Santa," Michael shouted. His head was spinning in the reality of all the terrific gifts that Santa had generously planted under his family's Christmas tree.

"This IS Christmas," Michael declared as he took a last trip up and down the hallway. On his final landing, he swooped right to the foot of the tree. With one great slide, he glided in on his knees, then belly, landing just under a branch.

He flipped his body, positioning himself right under the bobbing ornaments. There he lay, face to face with a blown-glass, red-faced Santa. "Thanks, Santa," Michael echoed. "This has been a Christmas to remember."

The red-faced Santa's stare was blank. In his cold
stone-faced paint there was no acceptance of
Michael's extravagant praise. His black eyes, white
beard, and mittened hands did not so much as
flinch as the tree branches gently repositioned
themselves.

Michael's hands opened, allowing the plane to glide
over and across his shoulder in a nose dive. It was
the flannel collar of his new holiday pajamas, the
ones with the space rockets, that interrupted his
morning madness. Something about the soft, warm
cloth carried Michael to another place and time.

Michael brought his hands to his face, thinking he could rub himself back into his current world. There was no remaining there. All attempts Michael had of staying in his own Christmas world were foiled.

His mind let go, his heart opened, and in his head were the images of the light filled stable from the night before.

Except this time the story played itself in reverse. First, the princes from the east brought treasures for the child and his family. Next, the shepherds and animals visited the meager manger. Finally, there was the baby in the manger.

The desire to stay here with this child amongst the simplicity of this world was intense. As Michael lay still on the floor in his home, he contemplated the infant who lay still on the straw of the manger.

"What gift could I bring?" thought Michael. He raced through his mind, recalling each of the gifts that he, himself, had received this day. The plane with its auto-effects and drop down landing gear?

"No, too noisy." The action figure with semi-automatic long gun? "No, that was not right either."

It did not seem to matter which gift he remembered, none would honor this Holy Child.

At once, Michael recalled the face of the gentleman carrying the last gift. He had seemed sad. No, not sad, something different. What it was, Michael could not describe, yet in his own heart he felt what the man's face spoke. "There is NO gift good enough to bring this child. Nothing I have is worthy."

With that, Michael's heart did speak. It spoke the
words that were more valuable than any gift of gold,
fine spices, or oil. From the depth of Michael's heart,
he said, "I love you, Jesus."

And for one very brief moment, across the bridge
of time, Michael saw the child from his vision turn
His face toward this boy under the tree,

and with all the love of Heaven, The young
Lord Jesus acknowledged Michael's words

and smiled.

Prophecies of Jesus' Coming:

Isaiah 7:14 (KJV) Therefore the Lord himself shall give you a sign; Behold, a virgin shall conceive, and bear a son, and shall call his name Immanuel.

Isaiah 9:6 (KJV) For unto us a child is born, unto us a son is given: and the government shall be upon his shoulder: and his name shall be called Wonderful, Counsellor, The mighty God, The everlasting Father, The Prince of Peace.

Micah 5:2 (KJV) But thou, Bethlehem Ephratah, though thou be little among the thousands of Judah, yet out of thee shall he come forth unto me that is to be ruler in Israel; whose goings forth have been from of old, from everlasting.

Isaiah 60: 3,6, 9 (KJV) 3 And the Gentiles shall come to thy light, and kings to the brightness of thy rising. 6 The multitude of camels shall cover thee, the dromedaries of Midian and Ephah; all they from Sheba shall come: they shall bring gold and incense; and they shall shew forth the praises of the LORD. 9 Surely the isles shall wait for me, and the ships of Tarshish first, to bring thy sons from far, their silver and their gold with them, unto the name of the LORD thy God, and to the Holy One of Israel, because he hath glorified thee.

Biblical Record of Jesus' Birth:
According to Luke:

Luke 1:26-38 (KJV)

26 And in the sixth month the angel Gabriel was sent from God unto a city of Galilee, named Nazareth, 27 To a virgin espoused to a man whose name was Joseph, of the house of David; and the virgin's name was Mary. 28 And the angel came in unto her, and said, Hail, thou that art highly favoured, the Lord is with thee: blessed art thou among women. 29 And when she saw him, she was troubled at his saying, and cast in her mind what manner of salutation this should be. 30 And the angel said unto her, Fear not, Mary: for thou hast found favour with God. 31 And, behold, thou shalt conceive in thy womb, and bring forth a son, and shalt call his name JESUS. 32 He shall be great, and shall be called the Son of the Highest: and the Lord God shall give unto him the throne of his father David: 33 And he shall reign over the house of Jacob for ever; and of his kingdom there shall be no end.
34 Then said Mary unto the angel, How shall this be, seeing I know not a man? 35 And the angel answered and said unto her, The Holy Ghost shall come upon thee, and the power of the Highest shall overshadow thee: therefore also that holy thing which shall be born of thee shall be called the Son of God.
36 And, behold, thy cousin Elisabeth, she hath also conceived a son in her old age: and this is the sixth month with her, who was called barren. 37 For with God nothing shall be impossible.
38 And Mary said, Behold the handmaid of the Lord; be it unto me according to thy word. And the angel departed from her.

Biblical Record of Jesus' Birth:
According to Luke:

Luke 2:1-20 (KJV)

1 And it came to pass in those days, that there went out a decree from Caesar Augustus, that all the world should be taxed. 2 (And this taxing was first made when Cyrenius was governor of Syria.) 3 And all went to be taxed, every one into his own city. 4 And Joseph also went up from Galilee, out of the city of Nazareth, into Judaea, unto the city of David, which is called Bethlehem; (because he was of the house and lineage of David:) 5 To be taxed with Mary his espoused wife, being great with child. 6 And so it was, that, while they were there, the days were accomplished that she should be delivered. 7 And she brought forth her first-born son, and wrapped him in swaddling clothes, and laid him in a manger; because there was no room for them in the inn. 8 And there were in the same country shepherds abiding in the field, keeping watch over their flock by night. 9 And, lo, the angel of the Lord came upon them, and the glory of the Lord shone round about them: and they were sore afraid. 10 And the angel said unto them, Fear not: for, behold, I bring you good tidings of great joy, which shall be to all people. 11 For unto you is born this day in the city of David a Saviour, which is Christ the Lord. 12 And this shall be a sign unto you; Ye shall find the babe wrapped in swaddling clothes, lying in a manger. 13 And suddenly there was with the angel a multitude of the heavenly host praising God, and saying, 14 Glory to God in the highest, and on earth peace, good will toward men. 15 And it came to pass, as the angels were gone away from them into heaven, the shepherds said one to another,

Biblical Record of Jesus' Birth:
According to Luke:

Luke 2:15-20 (KJV)

Let us now go even unto Bethlehem, and see this thing which is come to pass, which the Lord hath made known unto us. 16 And they came with haste, and found Mary, and Joseph, and the babe lying in a manger. 17 And when they had seen it, they made known abroad the saying which was told them concerning this child. 18 And all they that heard it wondered at those things which were told them by the shepherds. 19 But Mary kept all these things, and pondered them in her heart. 20 And the shepherds returned, glorifying and praising God for all the things that they had heard and seen, as it was told unto them.

Biblical Record of Jesus' Birth:
According to Matthew:

Matthew 2:1-12 (KJV)

1 Now when Jesus was born in Bethlehem of Judaea in the days of Herod the king, behold, there came wise men from the east to Jerusalem, 2 Saying, Where is he that is born King of the Jews? for we have seen his star in the east, and are come to worship him. 3 When Herod the king had heard these things, he was troubled, and all Jerusalem with him. 4 And when he had gathered all the chief priests and scribes of the people together, he demanded of them where Christ should be born. 5 And they said unto him, In Bethlehem of Judaea: for thus it is written by the prophet, 6 And thou Bethlehem, in the land of Juda, art not the least among the princes of Juda: for out of thee shall come a Governor, that shall rule my people Israel. 7 Then Herod, when he had privily called the wise men, enquired of them diligently what time the star appeared. 8 And he sent them to Bethlehem, and said, Go and search diligently for the young child; and when ye have found him, bring me word again, that I may come and worship him also.
9 When they had heard the king, they departed; and, lo, the star, which they saw in the east, went before them, till it came and stood over where the young child was. 10 When they saw the star, they rejoiced with exceeding great joy. 11 And when they were come into the house, they saw the young child with Mary his mother, and fell down, and worshipped him: and when they had opened their treasures, they presented unto him gifts; gold, and frankincense, and myrrh. 12 And being warned of God in a

Biblical Record of Jesus' Birth:
According to Matthew:

Matthew 2:12-15 (KJV)

dream that they should not return to Herod, they departed into their own country another way. 13 And when they were departed, behold, the angel of the Lord appeareth to Joseph in a dream, saying, Arise, and take the young child and his mother, and flee into Egypt, and be thou there until I bring thee word: for Herod will seek the young child to destroy him. 14 When he arose, he took the young child and his mother by night, and departed into Egypt: 15 And was there until the death of Herod: that it might be fulfilled which was spoken of the Lord by the prophet, saying, Out of Egypt have I called my son.

Made in the USA
Charleston, SC
20 December 2013